Read all the titles in this series

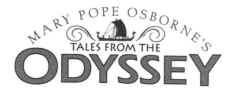

MARY POPE OSBORNE'S
TALES FROM THE
ODYSSEY

BOOK ONE
THE ONE-EYED GIANT

BOOK TWO
THE LAND OF THE DEAD

BOOK THREE
SIRENS AND SEA MONSTERS

BOOK FOUR
THE GRAY-EYED GODDESS

BOOK FIVE
RETURN TO ITHACA

Coming soon:
BOOK SIX
THE FINAL BATTLE

Circe's
Island

The
Sirens

Island of
Aeolus

Scylla

Cyclops'
Cave

Island of
the Sun God

Charybdis

Land of the Dead

Calypso's
Island

Land of the
Lotus Eaters

Oceanus

MAP OF ODYSSEUS' JOURNEY

GREECE

Troy

CRETE

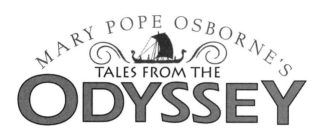

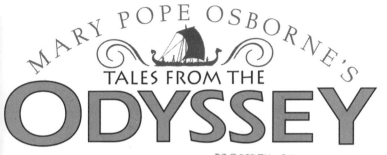

MARY POPE OSBORNE'S

TALES FROM THE

ODYSSEY

Book Five

RETURN TO ITHACA

By **MARY POPE OSBORNE**
With artwork by **TROY HOWELL**

Hyperion Paperbacks for Children   New York

For Chip Hughes

Special thanks to Frederick J. Booth, Ph.D.,
Professor of Classical Studies, Seton Hall University,
for his expert advice

Text copyright © 2004 by Mary Pope Osborne
Artwork copyright © 2004 by Troy Howell

First Hyperion Paperback edition, 2004
3 5 7 9 10 8 6 4 2
Printed in the United States of America

Library of Congress Cataloging-in-Publication Data on file.
ISBN 0-7868-0993-0 (pbk.)
Visit www.hyperionbooksforchildren.com

CONTENTS

PROLOGUE 7

1 ⸱⸱ SEPARATION AND SORROW 9

2 ⸱⸱ THE PRINCESS 15

3 ⸱⸱ THE STRANGER 22

4 ⸱⸱ THE FEAST 32

5 ⸱⸱ RETURN TO ITHACA 41

6 ⸱⸱ THE MYSTERIOUS SHEPHERD 50

7 ⸱⸱ THE SWINEHERD 60

8 ⸱⸱ RETURN OF THE SON 70

9 ⸱⸱ REUNION 77

10 ⸱⸱ A PLAN FOR REVENGE 88

ABOUT HOMER AND THE ODYSSEY 93

GODS AND GODDESSES
    OF ANCIENT GREECE 96

THE MAIN GODS AND GODDESSES
    AND PRONUNCIATION OF THEIR NAMES 98

PRONUNCIATION GUIDE
    TO OTHER PROPER NAMES 101

A NOTE ON THE SOURCES 103

ABOUT THE AUTHOR 105

PROLOGUE

*I*n the early morning of time, there existed a mysterious world called Mount Olympus. Hidden behind a veil of clouds, this world was never swept by winds, nor washed by rains. Those who lived on Mount Olympus never grew old; they never died. They were not humans. They were the mighty gods and goddesses of ancient Greece.

The Olympian gods and goddesses had great power over the lives of the humans who lived on earth below. Their anger once caused a man named Odysseus to wander the seas for many long years, trying to find his way home.

Almost three thousand years ago, a Greek poet named Homer first told the story of Odysseus' journey. Since that time, story-tellers have told the strange and wondrous tale again and again. We call that story the Odyssey.

ONE

SEPARATION AND SORROW

$\mathcal{B}$eneath an olive tree on a strange shore lay Odysseus, the lost king of Ithaca. In the weeks before, Odysseus had fought for his life against a terrible storm. He had lived many days without food or fresh water. He had narrowly escaped death with the aid of a sea goddess. And now, covered by a blanket of leaves, he was drifting into a deep and exhausted sleep.

For the twenty years since he had left the battlefields of Troy, Odysseus had tried desperately to return to his beloved island of Ithaca. In that time, he had braved many storms and fought many monsters. He had lost his fleet of twelve ships and all of his men.

Odysseus ached always to return to his home and be reunited with his wife,

Penelope, and their son, Telemachus. Though he had not seen them in twenty years, they were ever in his heart and mind. But as he lay on this distant shore, it seemed impossible to Odysseus that he would ever get home. . . .

※　　※　　※

As Odysseus slept on the beach, far away Penelope slept in her palace bed, weary from weeping. For many years, wicked men had invaded her husband's estate, demanding that she take one of them for a husband. Penelope had stead-fastly refused, and now her suitors were plotting to kill her son as he returned home from searching for his father. Upon hearing this news, Penelope had collapsed. She could hardly bear her husband's absence. Surely she would die if she lost her son as well. . . .

❁　❁　❁

Far away from Ithaca, Penelope's son, Telemachus, lay in a splendid chamber in the palace of the king and queen of Sparta. He had traveled there to find news of his father, and his quest had been fulfilled. King Menelaus had told him that Odysseus might be a captive on the island of the goddess Calypso.

Since receiving this news, Telemachus had been asking himself the same questions over and over: Should he set out in search of Calypso's island in hopes of finding his father? Or should he return to Ithaca and help his mother in her struggle against the suitors who were trying to take his father's place?

The son of Odysseus did not know that even now evil men were waiting to ambush him on his way home.

High on Mount Olympus, the gray-eyed goddess Athena looked down on Odysseus, Penelope, and Telemachus. Something must be done to save Odysseus and his wife and son, she thought—and quickly. So, in the hour before dawn, Athena left her bright, perfect world in the clouds and slipped down to the small and troubled world below. . . .

THE PRINCESS

*A*thena traveled swiftly over the earth to the land of King Alcinous. King Alcinous was a wise and generous leader, and his kingdom was blessed. The men were the best sailors in all the world, and the women were the best weavers.

Athena passed green fields, splendid temples, and lovely houses until finally she came to the palace of the king and queen. In the hour before dawn, she slipped through the entranceway, then down the hall to the chamber of the king's daughter, Nausicaa.

The goddess glided silently into the princess's room. Like a breath of wind, she swept past two young handmaidens sleeping near the door.

Athena hovered for a moment over the princess's bed. Then she quickly changed her shape to that of Nausicaa's closest friend. She spoke to the princess as if in a dream.

"Nausicaa, you are so lazy!" she said. "Don't you know that there are many dirty clothes in the palace that must be washed? How will you ever marry if you do not have a clean gown? At dawn, you must load the best linen into a wagon and go to the pools near the shore and do the washing!"

The gray-eyed goddess then slipped out of the palace as swiftly and silently as she had come.

When dawn broke, Nausicaa woke and remembered her strange dream. She hurried at once to her parents' chamber. "Father! I must go today and wash all our best clothes in the sea!" she said. "If I do not have clean clothes, how will I ever marry?"

King Alcinous smiled. He thought his daughter's words were strange, but he could refuse her nothing. "If that is what you wish, Nausicaa, that is what you shall do," he said. "I will tell the servants to fetch a wagon and harness the mules so you can carry all our clothes down to the sea."

The king's servants quickly prepared a wagon. The princess and her handmaidens loaded piles of soiled cloaks, robes, tunics, and gowns into the back. They packed a lunch of bread and meat, a goatskin filled with wine, and a flask of golden olive oil.

Nausicaa climbed into the driver's seat of the wagon and snapped the reins. The team of mules lunged forward and the wagon rattled noisily over the road, carrying the princess and her handmaidens toward the sea.

When they came to the washing pools

near the shore, the girls unhitched the mules. They unloaded the wagon and carried the piles of clothes down to the pools. They stamped on the garments, washing them in seawater until they were spotless. Then they spread them over the rocks to dry.

As they waited for the sun and wind to dry their laundry, the princess and her handmaidens bathed in the sea. They ate their bread and meat. Then they threw off their veils and began playing ball.

The princess tossed the ball high into the air. A maiden missed the catch, and the ball rolled into the water. As the girls ran to get it, they laughed and shouted.

Not far away, a sad and weary man lay beneath a blanket of leaves under an olive tree. When he heard the voices of the young girls, he opened his eyes.

Where am I? he wondered. *Who is shouting and laughing? Their voices sound like those of nymphs who haunt rivers and mountains.*

Odysseus broke off a bough of thick leaves to hide his nakedness. Then he crept out from under the olive tree into the afternoon sun.

THREE

THE STRANGER

When the handmaidens saw Odysseus, they screamed and ran away. But Princess Nausicaa stood very still, for Athena had filled her heart with courage. The young girl stared at the unkempt stranger, covered with sea salt and dirt and leaves.

"Beautiful princess, are you a goddess or a mortal?" Odysseus said. "Whoever you are, have pity on me, for I have suffered much. I was tossed upon the seas for twenty days, until the waves flung me onto this shore. Can you give me clothes to hide my nakedness? Can you tell me the way to your town?"

The princess drew close to Odysseus. "Stranger, I believe you are a good man," she said. "I am Nausicaa, the daughter of King Alcinous. My maids and I will help you."

Nausicaa called for her handmaidens to come out of their hiding places. She ordered them to bring clean clothes and olive oil for the mysterious stranger.

Odysseus washed himself in a stream, then rubbed the olive oil over his battered, sun-dried skin. When he had dressed himself in a tunic and cloak, the princess's handmaidens brought him meat and wine.

After Odysseus finished his meal, Princess Nausicaa told him what he must do. "You may follow our wagon to the walls of the town," she said, "but when we get inside the walls, you must leave us. The men of my land are the finest sailors in the world, but they are suspicious of strangers. They may think you are a vagabond from some foreign ship and speak ill of me for leading you to our city."

"Where should I go?" asked Odysseus.

"Inside the walls of the city there is a grove of poplars sacred to Athena. Wait there until I have had time to get home," said Nausicaa. "Then come to the palace. Inside you will find my parents sitting before a fire. My mother will be spinning dark-blue wool. Kneel before her and ask for help."

The princess then shook the reins of her wagon, and the mules began clattering toward town.

Odysseus followed the wagon past fields and farmland and a harbor filled with fine ships. When the wagon arrived at the narrow gates of the city, Odysseus followed it through the gates, then stopped and watched it rattle on without him.

Odysseus walked quickly through a marketplace filled with merchants selling fish, sails, and ship's oars. As he made his way between the stalls, several of the merchants and customers eyed him suspiciously. Odysseus quickly slipped past them and into the sacred grove of poplar trees. He hid among the trees, waiting for the princess to reach the palace.

While he waited, Odysseus prayed to the gods. "Hear me, O gods of Olympus! Have pity upon me," he begged. "Grant that I may make my way safely to the palace and find favor with the king and queen."

Odysseus remained hidden in the olive grove until he was sure Princess Nausicaa had had enough time to reach the palace.

Then he stepped cautiously out onto the city streets again.

As Odysseus started out of the grove, a strange mist covered his body. No one seemed to notice him as he made his way through the streets. *Has Athena made me invisible?* he wondered.

Suddenly a small girl stepped in front of Odysseus. The child stared up at him with bright gray eyes. Odysseus wondered if the girl might be Athena in disguise.

"Can you tell me the way to the palace of the king?" he asked her.

"I will show you," said the child. "Follow me and speak to no one."

Odysseus followed the girl through the streets. When they drew near the palace, she said simply, "Go inside and look for the queen." Then she disappeared, leaving Odysseus alone at the palace gates.

Odysseus entered the gates and passed through an orchard of trees laden with luscious figs, pears, and apples. He walked through a rich vineyard and a bountiful flower garden.

When he entered the halls of the palace, he gasped in wonder. The palace shone with a splendor like that of the sun and moon. Golden statues of boys holding fiery torches lit the halls. In the gleaming light, handmaidens worked at their looms. Their fingers fluttered like aspen leaves in the wind as they wove their beautiful linen.

No one seemed to notice Odysseus as he walked through the palace. Hidden by Athena's cloak of mist, he slipped silently into the great hall. As Odysseus looked about for the queen, he saw a group of nobles sitting near an open fire. Nearby sat the king and a woman spinning wool.

Odysseus moved quickly toward Nausicaa's mother. As he knelt in the ashes before the hearth, he felt the mist around him evaporate—and suddenly, he was visible again.

Some in the hall cried out in alarm when they saw the strange, haggard man. But Odysseus spoke quickly and passionately to the queen: "I humbly beg you to have pity on me!" he said. "I have come here from beyond the sea. Help me find my way back to my home country, to my wife and my son."

THE FEAST

*E*veryone in the great hall stared in shock at Odysseus as he knelt before the queen. Finally an old man broke the silence. "We must honor our most ancient tradition," he said. "Almighty Zeus tells us never to deny a stranger who asks for our protection. Give this wretched man a chair. Offer him wine and supper."

King Alcinous helped Odysseus to a chair. A servant brought a silver basin and washed Odysseus' hands. Others brought him bread and meat and wine.

The king and queen and all their guests raised their cups in the air. "To Zeus, protector of worthy strangers," said the king. Then he looked at Odysseus. "Perhaps you are one of the immortals yourself, come down to earth to test our hospitality."

Odysseus shook his head. "Pray, sir, do not mistake me for a god. In truth, I am the most wretched of men. If only you knew what misery I have suffered."

King Alcinous seemed moved by Odysseus' humble words. He turned to his guests. "Go safely to your homes now. Tomorrow we will honor this traveler with a feast."

When the guests had all taken their leave and Odysseus was left alone with the king and queen, the queen spoke gently to him. "I see that you do not wear your own clothes, my friend," she said, "for those are garments that my daughter took to the washing pools this morning. You say that you have come from beyond the sea. In truth, who are you? Where is your home?"

Odysseus did not want to reveal his true identity. So he told them only of leaving the island of Calypso and escaping the terrible storm. He told them about their daughter's kindness toward him.

Satisfied with his story, the queen ordered her servants to prepare a room for Odysseus. He was soon led to his bed, where he lay down on soft purple blankets. As soon as the torches were put out, he fell into a deep, restful sleep.

⁂

The next morning, palace servants set about preparing a great feast. They roasted sheep, boars, and oxen. A messenger was sent to summon the finest singer in the land, a blind minstrel.

As King Alcinous' servants made preparations for the feast, Athena walked through the streets of the city. Disguised as the king's herald, she called to every citizen: "Come, lords and princes! Come hear the stories of the stranger who has arrived at the palace of the king!"

A great crowd gathered at the palace for the feast. When King Alcinous brought Odysseus before his people, the crowd gasped. Odysseus could see great wonder in their faces. Though he was still weary from his ordeal at sea, he suspected that Athena had made him look tall and strong and given him an air of great dignity.

As the feasting began, the blind singer sat down by a pillar and cradled his harp in his arms. Soon the spirit moved him, and he began singing about famous warriors who had died in battle. He sang about the heroes of the Trojan War, about brave Achilles and King Agamemnon.

As the singer sang, Odysseus wept for his lost friends. He hid his face behind his robe, so none could see his tears. He did not want them to guess who he really was.

But later, after sports and games, Odysseus felt merry and confident. He called out to the singer: "Sing about the wooden horse that helped the Greeks win the war! If you tell the true story of the fall of Troy, I will praise your storytelling the whole world over!"

The singer began singing about a Greek king named Odysseus. He sang about how Odysseus had ordered the making of a giant wooden horse, and how he had hidden himself inside the horse with his finest warriors. He sang about how the Trojans had brought the horse inside the walls of Troy, and how the Greeks, led by Odysseus, had crept out at nightfall and laid siege to the city, and thus won the war.

As the minstrel sang, Odysseus began

to weep again. This time, he could not hide his grief. He wept uncontrollably.

King Alcinous ordered the singer to silence his harp. "Our guest has wept twice today when you sang about the Trojan War," he said. "I imagine your songs have stirred his memories." Then the king turned to Odysseus. "Sir, do not try to hide what you feel or who you are any longer," he said. "Tell us your name. Tell us about your travels and what you have seen. Did you see the fall of Troy? Did your friends perish in battle? I ask you to tell us your story."

FIVE

RETURN TO ITHACA

Odysseus stood and faced the crowd. "Where should I begin?" he said. "I have such a long, sad tale to tell. First, I will tell you my name: I am Odysseus. My home is Ithaca, a bright and beautiful island. The island is low and the water around it can often be rough. But there is no sight more beautiful than one's own home. I have not seen my island or my family for twenty years, not since I sailed away to fight the Trojan War. . . ."

Odysseus went on to tell how the Greeks had fought for ten years in faraway Troy—and how their mighty fleet had set sail for home after winning the war. He told how a terrible storm had driven his twelve ships off course and sent them to the Land of the Lotus Eaters—and then to the cave of the hideous Cyclops monster.

Odysseus told about the horror of seeing the giant one-eyed monster eat his warriors alive—and how he had led his men in a daring escape by hiding in the fleece of the monster's rams.

Odysseus told how the Wind God had given him a bag of winds to help speed his ships home. And how, when they were within sight of Ithaca, his men had disobeyed his orders and opened the bag while he was sleeping, releasing a terrible gale that swept their ships back across the sea, far away from home.

Odysseus told how cannibal giants had murdered most of his men and sunk eleven of his twelve ships. He told how he and his crew had then sailed to the island of Circe, the enchantress, and how the beautiful witch had turned his men into pigs. He told about his journey to the mist-filled Land of the Dead, where he saw the ghosts of friends who had died, and, the saddest sight of all, the ghost of his own mother.

Odysseus told how his ship sailed past the Sirens, the strange bird-women who lured sailors to watery death with their beautiful singing. He told how his ship was forced to pass between two deadly creatures—the hideous six-headed monster, Scylla, and the whirlpool monster, Charybdis.

Odysseus told how his men had disobeyed the gods and slain the cattle of the Sun God—and how, for this offense, the gods had drowned the last of his men in a horrible storm at sea.

Odysseus told how he had then sailed alone to the island of Calypso—and how the goddess had kept him prisoner for seven long years. He told about leaving her island and clinging to a raft for twenty days and nights at sea, until he had finally crawled upon the very shores where Princess Nausicaa and her hand-maidens had found him.

At the end of his astonishing tale, Odysseus sighed with sorrow. "I want now only to return to my family," he said. "I want to go home."

All who had listened to Odysseus' story were silent with awe. At long last the king spoke: "For many years, this man has been far from his native island, and now he asks only that we help him return to his family. Tomorrow, fifty-two of our finest sailors will prepare a ship, and at sunset, we will send him on his way home."

❦　❦　❦

The next day, King Alcinous' servants packed a great ship with fine clothes and gifts of gold. As the sun sank low in the sky, the king's men sacrificed an ox to Zeus, almighty ruler on Mount Olympus.

"May the gods always bless your family for your great kindness and generosity," Odysseus said to the king.

The ship's sailors then laid a blanket on the deck for Odysseus. They urged him to lie on the blanket and take his rest as they set sail. In silence, Odysseus lay down on the blanket and closed his eyes.

The crew took their places. They raised their anchor and began to row. As the ship moved through the twilight, Odysseus fell asleep. After years of struggling against the ills of war, against storms and hideous monsters, he struggled no more.

The king's ship sped like a team of galloping stallions over the sea. Even falcons could not keep up with her as she moved across the purple waves.

In the hour before dawn, the ship drew close to an island harbor. Bordered by steep slopes, the harbor was free of wild winds. Its waters were calm.

The crew dropped anchor and leaped ashore. Odysseus did not stir from his slumber. The sailors wrapped the sleeping warrior in his blanket and gently carried him onto the sand. There they left him, sleeping peacefully in the shade of an olive tree. They placed his gifts near him on the sand: bronze cauldrons, golden plates, and richly woven garments. Then they returned to their ship and set sail.

After twenty long years, Odysseus of Ithaca was finally home.

SIX

THE MYSTERIOUS
SHEPHERD

When Odysseus awoke, he found himself surrounded by a mist. Through the haze, he saw strange winding paths and ghostly high cliffs. Nothing looked familiar. When he saw the gifts from the king piled near him, he fell into despair.

Why did King Alcinous order his men to sail to this place? he wondered. *Why have they abandoned me here?*

Odysseus paced up and down the beach, angry at the king for sending him to an unknown shore. When he saw a young shepherd coming toward him, he rushed to meet him.

"Greetings, friend!" Odysseus shouted through the mist. "I beg you not to fear me, but to tell me the truth—where am I? What country is this?"

"Sir, you must be a stranger to this region, if you do not know this island," said the shepherd. "It is known far and wide, from the glow of dawn to the gloom of twilight. It is a rugged place, not good for horses, but it grows grain and grapes. It receives plenty of rain, so it has good water and good grass for goats and cattle. Even those who have traveled from as far away as Troy know the island's name: it is Ithaca."

Odysseus could not believe his ears. *Surely, I would recognize my own country,* he thought. He feared the shepherd might be trying to trick him, so he quickly invented a story.

"Ah, yes, I thought so," he said, "I myself came here to Ithaca to escape punishment for killing a thief who tried to steal my treasure from the Trojan War." He pointed to the gleaming gifts on the sand.

The shepherd smiled. Then, in the wink of an eye, the young man was transformed into a tall, striking woman with gray, glinting eyes.

"Athena," breathed Odysseus.

"Odysseus, you are the world's most cunning storyteller," she said. "But still you did not know me, your guardian and protector. I have come here to help you again. I did not want others to see you, so I again shrouded you in a mist. It made your surroundings look unfamiliar to you. But never fear, this is indeed your homeland."

"Goddess, how do I know you are telling me the truth?" said Odysseus. How can I know that I have really come home?"

Athena waved her wand. "Look about you now, Odysseus," she said, "and you will see the olive trees with their long leaves. You will see the dusky cave where nymphs weave their sea-purple webs. You will see the springs that never run dry. Behold—Ithaca." As she said these words, the goddess dispersed the mist that surrounded them.

In the bright, clear air, Odysseus saw all the things the goddess had described. Joyfully he fell to his knees and kissed the ground.

"Come," said Athena, "let us hide these treasures in the cave of the nymphs. Then we will make a plan."

Together Odysseus and Athena stowed

the gold and bronze and woven clothes in the cave. Then Athena rolled a stone over the cave's entrance.

When the stone was in place and the treasures were safe, Athena and Odysseus sat on the ground beneath an olive tree. There Athena told him all about the suitors who had invaded his home.

"For several years, Penelope fought off the evil men," she said. "Finally, she promised to choose one to marry, but she never intended to do so. One of her maids reported her deceit and the suitors raged against her. Now time is running out. She mourns for you but does not give up hope."

Odysseus fought to contain his anger against those who had tormented his faithful wife. He quietly asked the goddess to help him. "Tell me what to do," he said. "Give me courage. With your help, I can fight three hundred men."

"You will fight them," said Athena. "But now, you must tell no one who you are. Suffer all you hear and see in silence, until you can take your revenge."

"But might not some of my countrymen recognize me?" said Odysseus.

"I will see to it that they do not," said Athena. "I will disguise you as an old man. I will take the hair from your head and wrinkle your flesh and dim your eyes. I will give you rags to wear, like those worn by a wretched beggar."

With these words, Athena raised her wand and passed it over Odysseus. She shriveled the smooth skin that covered his body. She took the hair from his head and the light from his eyes. She draped a ragged cloak about his shoulders and gave him a walking stick and a tattered bag.

"Be on your way now," the goddess said. "Go to the hut of your swineherd. He is a good and honest man. Stay with him while I go to Telemachus. I will bring him home from the sea where he seeks some sign that you are still alive."

"O goddess, why did you let my son drift in despair, searching for me?" asked Odysseus. "Why did you not tell him the truth?"

"Do not fear, I was with him for much of his journey," said Athena. "And even though evildoers plot to murder him, I promise you—*they* will soon die instead."

SEVEN

THE SWINEHERD

*O*dysseus leaned on his walking stick and trod slowly over the stony path that led away from the sea. He hobbled through the woods and over the hills to his estate.

Finally Odysseus came upon the swineherd who had long tended his hundreds of hogs. The old man sat in front of a crude stone shelter near the swine pens. He was making a pair of leather sandals. Near him lay four savage dogs that guarded the hogs.

When the dogs caught sight of Odysseus, they lunged forward, snarling and growling.

Odysseus threw down his stick and crouched on the ground. The swineherd rushed forward, shouting and throwing stones at the vicious dogs, driving them away.

"You are lucky, old man," the swineherd said to Odysseus. "In another minute, they might have killed you. Stand and come into my hut. I will give you food and wine. Then you can tell me your story—from where you have come, and what sorrows you have known."

Keeping the dogs at bay, the swineherd led Odysseus inside his simple hut. He made a seat of soft twigs, covered it with a shaggy goatskin, and invited Odysseus to sit down.

"You are kind, sir," said Odysseus. "May mighty Zeus bless you for your hospitality. May he grant your greatest wish."

"I have only one wish—that my dear master was still alive," said the swineherd. "Had he lived he would surely have given me a reward for caring tenderly for his livestock these many years. He might have given me a house, a wife, and a piece of land. But alas, my good master has been gone for twenty years. He died far away from home, returning from the war with Troy. Storm spirits destroyed his ships and all his men."

"And what of his family?" Odysseus asked softly.

"Ah, his wife waits for him in vain, while other men try to force her to marry. His mother gave up hope of his return long ago and died of grief. His father wishes to die now also—the old man no longer lives in the palace, but sleeps alone in the vineyards. As for the son of Odysseus—the poor boy wanders the earth, looking for his father. It is tragic indeed."

The faithful swineherd sighed deeply, then stood up. "Let me feed you now, good sir," he said.

The swineherd set about preparing a meal for Odysseus. He served him meat still hot on the spit and sprinkled with barley meal. He gave him wine in a cup made from ivy wood.

As they ate and drank together, the swineherd complained to Odysseus about Penelope's suitors. "They butcher the best hogs of the farm," he said. "They slaughter the cattle and rob the storehouses and drink my master's wine. Worst of all, they torment my poor mistress night and day, demanding that she forget Odysseus and marry one of them.

Ah, but she is faithful beyond compare. She weeps for her lost husband and will not give up hope for his return."

"Do her suitors not heed her wishes?" asked Odysseus.

"Nay, these men will not leave her alone! They are cruel and without pity. I hear rumors that they now lie in wait, plotting to murder her son."

Odysseus said nothing. But in his mind, he coldly brooded upon revenge, and the seeds of the suitors' deaths were sown.

As Odysseus and the swineherd

finished their meal, a storm began to blow outside. Wind and rain pelted the roof of the small hut. The swineherd gave Odysseus more wine and asked him to tell about himself.

Odysseus lied. He said that he was born in Crete and had wandered many towns until he had come to Ithaca. "But I must tell you this," he said, "on my travels, I met a king who told me that Odysseus of Ithaca is still alive. The king said Odysseus will return home on a dark night, when the new moon is hidden. He said he might return openly or he might return in secret."

The swineherd shook his head sadly. "Do not try to raise my hopes, friend," he said. "In the past, other wanderers have passed through Ithaca with rumors about Odysseus. Each time, they have tormented his poor wife with their falsehoods. Again and again she has imagined that she might soon see her husband. Long ago, I myself believed a man who told me that my master would return in summer or in autumn. But Odysseus has never come back—and never will. I am certain that the fish have devoured him by now, and his bones lie deep in the sand of some far-away place."

As rainy darkness descended upon the stone hut, the swineherd made Odysseus a bed of sheepskins. He spread a thick cloak over him.

Then the faithful servant wrapped himself in the hide of a goat and left the hut. He went out into the dark, windy night and lay under the shelter of a rock, guarding his master's swine.

EIGHT

RETURN OF THE SON

While Odysseus had been making his way home to Ithaca, his son Telemachus had stayed on as a guest in the palace of the king and queen of Sparta.

For many days, Telemachus had wondered what to do. One night, as he tossed restlessly in bed, the goddess Athena appeared in his chambers.

Before Telemachus could speak, Athena gave him urgent advice: "Linger here no longer, Telemachus. Go home at once and protect your house. But beware—your mother's suitors plan to kill you. Right now, they wait to ambush you in the strait between Ithaca and the island of Samos."

"What should I do?" asked Telemachus.

"Sail quickly through this passage, hugging neither shore," said Athena. "The gods will send a fair wind to speed your ship on to a safe port. When you land, send your crew to town. Then go alone to your father's swineherd, the man who tends his hogs. Send him to your mother to tell her of your safe return."

Before Telemachus could ask more questions, Athena vanished from the room. Telemachus dressed hurriedly, then ran to King Menelaus' chambers. "My lord, I am sorry to take leave of you so soon, but I must set off for home immediately."

The king hated to see the son of Odysseus leave Sparta, but he consented and ordered that a chariot be prepared for him.

As Telemachus said farewell to King Menelaus and Queen Helen, a strange sight appeared in the sky. An eagle flew overhead. It clutched a great white goose in its talons.

Men and women ran across the fields. They pointed at the weird sight and cried out in amazement and fear.

"What omen is this?" someone shouted. "What can it mean?"

Queen Helen calmly answered. "The gods have revealed to my heart the meaning of this sign," she said. "The eagle stands for Odysseus. The goose stands for his home. After he has traveled far and wide, Odysseus will return home to Ithaca and take his revenge."

"May the gods make it so," said Telemachus. With that, the son of Odysseus snapped the reins of the horses and began his long journey home.

Telemachus' chariot raced across the plains of Sparta, then on to the harbor of Pylos. There Telemachus found his crew and ship waiting for him. He quickly boarded the vessel and ordered his men to raise the sail. Athena sent a fair west wind to start them on their way.

On their journey, Telemachus was careful to heed Athena's advice. He ordered his men not to sail close to either shore when they passed through the strait between Ithaca and the island of Samos.

As the black ship sped safely toward his home, Telemachus remembered more words from the goddess: *"When you land in Ithaca, send your crew to town. Then go alone to your father's swineherd, the man who tends his hogs. . . ."*

Just before they reached the port of Ithaca, Telemachus ordered his crew to strike their sail and row to land. When the ship was anchored, the crew went ashore and made a fire to cook their meat.

After all his men had eaten their fill, Telemachus spoke to them. "Now, row on to the city's port without me," he said. "I must travel alone and seek out my father's swineherd."

Once the men had cast off and the ship was on its way, Telemachus laced his fine leather sandals and picked up his mighty bronze spear. With rapid steps, he headed for the farmstead where the swineherd kept watch over the hogs.

NINE

REUNION

*M*orning was breaking over the swineherd's hut. The swineherd had built a fire and was preparing breakfast for himself and Odysseus. As he poured their wine, the dogs began yelping outside.

"Your dogs sound happy—they do not snarl or growl," Odysseus said to the swineherd. "They must be greeting someone they know and trust."

Before Odysseus could say more, a young man appeared in the doorway of the hut.

The swineherd jumped up, dropping the cups of wine. He ran to the young man and tearfully kissed him. "Telemachus! My eyes' sweet light!" the old man said.

Odysseus gazed upon his son's handsome face. He was unable to move or speak. When he had last seen his beloved boy, Telemachus had been a baby. Now he was a young man with broad shoulders and a proud chest, reddish hair, and lively, bright eyes. Indeed, he looked very like his father.

Telemachus smiled at the swineherd. "You are a welcome sight to my eyes, too!" he said. "Tell me first—how is my mother? What has happened to her since I left?"

"Word came to her that you were in grave danger," said the swineherd. "She will be overjoyed to hear that you have found your way home alive.

Come inside. Eat and rest."

As Telemachus drew near the hearth, Odysseus rose silently from his seat and offered it to his son.

Telemachus shook his head. "Keep your seat, old man," he said. "Another will serve me as well."

Odysseus nodded and took his place again. His face half hidden by the hood of his cloak, he continued to gaze with wonder upon the young man.

The swineherd threw fresh logs on the fire and spread a fleece on the ground for Telemachus. Then he prepared meat from the previous night's meal and a basket of bread. He served honeyed wine in wooden cups.

When the three men had finished their meal, Telemachus spoke softly to the swineherd. "Tell me, where does your guest come from?" he said. "What ship and what crew brought him here?"

"He comes from Crete and has traveled over the world. I put him in your hands now. Offer him the hospitality of your father's house."

Telemachus shook his head sadly. "How can I take a guest into our house when it is overrun by my mother's suitors? I can only offer him gifts. I will clothe him in a cloak and tunic and give him fine sandals and a sword and send him wherever he wants to go. But for now, I will visit with him, while you hurry to my mother and tell her of my safe return."

The swineherd nodded and stood up.

"Speak to her in secret," said Telemachus. "Let no one else know I am here."

"I understand," said the swineherd. Then he took his leave of Telemachus and Odysseus and set off for the palace.

After the swineherd had left, Odysseus saw a tall, fair woman appear in the doorway of the hut. Telemachus seemed not to take notice of her, but the dogs whimpered and cowered in fear.

The woman beckoned to Odysseus. He quietly left the fire and stepped outside. He followed her to a stone wall. Facing the woman in the morning light, Odysseus saw that it was the goddess Athena.

"Odysseus, it is time to tell your son the truth," the goddess said. "Then the two of you must plan your revenge on the suitors and make your way to town together. I will follow closely behind. I am ready for a fight."

Athena touched Odysseus with her wand. Instantly, the ragged garments fell away from his body and he was clad in a fine tunic and cloak. He was taller and looked much younger. His face was bronzed; his cheeks full. He had dark hair and a dark beard.

Athena had restored Odysseus to his strongest, most vital self. Before Odysseus could speak, the goddess vanished in the morning light.

Odysseus returned to the hut. When Telemachus saw him, a look of wonder and fear came over his face. He could barely speak. "Stranger—you have changed!" he stammered. "You must be a god from Mount Olympus! Spare me harm—allow me to make a sacrifice to you!"

Odysseus spoke quietly. "I am no god, Telemachus," he said. "I am the one you have mourned for, the one for whom you have suffered great pain and injury. I am your father."

The tears that Odysseus had long held

back now streamed down his face. But Telemachus shook his head. "No—you cannot be my father—you are a demon casting a spell, or you are a god. You were an old man, and now you are young—"

"I am not an immortal," said Odysseus, "but I have been blessed by a goddess. After twenty years of wandering and torment, Athena has brought me home to Ithaca. She changed me into an old man, and now I am a young man once more. It is easy for the gods to cast a man down and then raise him up again."

Hearing these words, Telemachus

began to weep. He grabbed his father and hugged him, and the two sobbed together. Their cries were wild and piercing, like those of eagles whose young have been stolen from them. After twenty long years, father and son were finally reunited.

A PLAN FOR REVENGE

Sitting together in the swineherd's hut, Odysseus and Telemachus asked many questions of each other. "What ship brought you here, Father?" said Telemachus. "Where is your crew?"

Odysseus told how King Alcinous had sent him home with the help of the best sailors in the world. "I slept all through the voyage," he said, "only to wake and find myself alone on shore, surrounded by gold and bronze treasure. With the help of Athena, I hid everything in the cave of the nymphs. Then Athena sent me here to find you. She wishes us now to plot revenge against our enemies."

"It may be hard for us to fight all of them," said Telemachus. "We are only two, and they number nearly one hundred and twenty."

"I believe Athena will help us," said Odysseus, "as will her father, Zeus. Do you think we will then be strong enough?"

"With the help of Zeus and Athena, we will surely defeat our enemies," said Telemachus. "Tell me what we must do."

"Tomorrow at daybreak, you must go home alone," said Odysseus. "I will disguise myself as a beggar again and travel to the palace. Do not protest if the suitors abuse me when I arrive. Even if they shout names at me or throw things at me, do not speak a word in my favor."

"When will we fight them?" asked Telemachus.

"When Athena whispers to me that the time has come, I will nod to you. You must then take all the swords and spears and shields from the hall and hide them in an upstairs room."

"What will I tell the others when they ask why I am doing this?" asked Telemachus.

"Say that you are removing the weapons so they will not be harmed from the smoke of the fires. Leave weapons only for you and me—two swords, two spears, and two leather shields. And remember, my son—tell no one that you have seen me—not the swineherd, nor any of the servants, nor my old father, not even your mother. . . ."

As the day wore on, Odysseus and Telemachus made further plans. Though Odysseus had finally returned to Ithaca, he knew he could still not rest. There was one more great battle to fight—but this one he would fight with his son.

ABOUT HOMER AND THE ODYSSEY

Long ago, the ancient Greeks believed that the world was ruled by a number of powerful gods and goddesses. Stories about the gods and goddesses are called the Greek myths. The myths were probably first told as a way to explain things in nature—such as weather, volcanoes, and constellations. They were also recited as entertainment.

The first written record of the Greek myths comes from a blind poet named Homer. Homer lived almost three thousand years ago. Many believe that Homer was the author of the world's two most famous epic poems: the *Iliad* and the *Odyssey*. The *Iliad* is the story of the Trojan War. The *Odyssey* tells about the long journey of Odysseus, king of an island called Ithaca. The tale concerns Odysseus' adventures on his way home from the Trojan War.

To tell his tales, Homer seems to have drawn upon a combination of his own imagination and Greek myths that had been passed down by word of mouth. A bit of actual history may have also gone into Homer's stories; there is archaeological evidence to suggest that the story of the Trojan War was based on a war fought about five hundred years before Homer's time.

Over the centuries, Homer's *Odyssey* has greatly influenced the literature of the Western world.

GODS AND GODDESSES OF ANCIENT GREECE

$\mathcal{T}$he most powerful of all the Greek gods and goddesses was Zeus, the thunder god. Zeus ruled the heavens and the mortal world from a misty mountaintop known as Mount Olympus. The main Greek gods and goddesses were all relatives of Zeus. His brother Poseidon was ruler of the seas, and his brother Hades was ruler of the underworld. His wife

Hera was queen of the gods and god-desses. Among his many children were the gods Apollo, Mars, and Hermes, and the goddesses Aphrodite, Athena, and Artemis.

The gods and goddesses of Mount Olympus not only inhabited their mountaintop but also visited the earth, involving themselves in the daily activities of mortals such as Odysseus.

THE MAIN GODS
AND GODDESSES
AND PRONUNCIATION
OF THEIR NAMES

Zeus (zyoos), king of the gods, god of thunder

Poseidon (poh-SY-don), brother of Zeus, god of seas and rivers

Hades (HAY-deez), brother of Zeus, king of the Land of the Dead

Hera (HEE-ra), wife of Zeus, queen of the Olympian gods and goddesses

Hestia (HES-tee-ah), sister of Zeus, goddess of the hearth

Athena (ah-THEE-nah), daughter of Zeus, goddess of wisdom and war, arts and crafts

Demeter (dih-MEE-tur), goddess of crops and the harvest, mother of Persephone

Aphrodite (ah-froh-DY-tee), daughter of Zeus, goddess of love and beauty

Artemis (AR-tem-is), daughter of Zeus, goddess of the hunt

Ares (AIR-eez), son of Zeus, god of war

Apollo (ah-POL-oh), god of the sun, music, and poetry

Hermes (HUR-meez), son of Zeus, messenger god, a trickster

Hephaestus (heh-FEES-tus), son of Hera, god of the forge

Persephone (pur-SEF-uh-nee), daughter of Zeus, wife of Hades and queen of the Land of the Dead

Dionysus (dy-oh-NY-sus), god of wine and madness

PRONUNCIATION GUIDE TO OTHER PROPER NAMES

Achilles (ah-KIL-ees)

Agamemnon (ag-ah-MEM-non)

Alcinous (al-SIN-oh-us)

Calypso (cah-LIP-soh)

Charybdis (kah-RIB-dis)

Circe (SIR-see)

Crete (KREET)

Cyclops (SY-klops)

Ithaca (ITH-ah-kah)

Menelaus (men-eh-LAY-us)

Nausicaa (now-SIK-eye-ah)

Odysseus (oh-DIS-yoos)

Penelope (pen-EL-oh-pee)

Pylos (PY-lohs)

Samos (SAH-moss)

Scylla (SIL-ah)

Sparta (SPAR-tah)

Telemachus (Tel-EM-ah-kus)

Trojans (TROH-junz)

A NOTE ON THE SOURCES

The story of the Odyssey was originally written down in the ancient Greek language. Since that time there have been countless translations of Homer's story into other languages. I consulted a number of English translations, including those written by Alexander Pope, Samuel Butler, Andrew Lang, W.H.D. Rouse, Edith Hamilton, Robert Fitzgerald, Allen Mandelbaum, and Robert Fagles.

Homer's *Odyssey* is divided into twenty-four books. The fifth volume of *Tales from the Odyssey* was derived from books 6, 7, 8, 13, 14, 15, 16 (with brief references to the events that take place in books 9-12).

ABOUT THE AUTHOR

MARY POPE OSBORNE is the author of the best-selling Magic Tree House series. She has also written many acclaimed historical novels and retellings of myths and folktales, including *Kate and the Beanstalk* and *New York's Bravest*. She lives with her husband in Connecticut.

Zeus

Hera

Artemis

Hephaestus

Apollo

Athena

Ares

GODS and GODDESSES of ANCIENT GREECE

Hermes

Dionysus

Aphrodite

Hestia

Demeter

Persephone

Poseidon

Hades